big NATE

WHAT'S A LITTLE NOOGIE BETWEEN FRIENDS?

by LINCOLN PEIRCE

TWEEE!

PENALTY KICK!
SORRY, BOYS.
NO WORRIES, TEDDY!

I'M AN EXPERT AT SAVING PENALTY KICKS!

I HAVE A KNACK FOR KNOWING EXACTLY WHAT THE SHOOTER'S GOING TO DO!

LIKE THIS GUY, FOR INSTANCE. IT'S SO OBVIOUS!

HE WANTS ME TO THINK HE'S GOING UPPER RIGHT...

...WHEN HE'S GOING LOWER LEFT!

TONG!

I PSYCHED HIM OUT.
NICELY DONE.
Peirce

BIG DAY TODAY, BOYS!
YES, AND **THIS** YEAR BETTER BE DIFFERENT!

I DON'T WANT A REPEAT OF **LAST** YEAR!

HA
HA HA
OHHHH, YEAH!
LAST YEAR!
HA HA
HA
HEH HEH
HA

HA HA HA HA HA HA HA HA
I HATE SCHOOL PICTURE DAY.

WHAT EXPRESSION SHOULD I USE FOR MY PICTURE, GUYS? HERE'S CHOICE A...
SCHOOL PIC

HERE'S B...

...AND HERE'S C.

I'D GO WITH "NONE OF THE ABOVE."
I LIKE **THAT** ONE!

HI, SCHOOL PICTURE GUY!
WHAT'S UP, KID? READY TO MAKE SOME PHOTO MAGIC?

YEAH, AS LONG AS YOU DON'T DO WHAT YOU DID LAST YEAR.
MOI? WHAT'D I DO?

YOU TOOK MY PICTURE WHEN I WASN'T READY! I LOOKED LIKE I WAS BRAIN-DEAD!

I WAS LIKE: NYURRR...
KLIK!
Peirce

YOU DID IT AGAIN! YOU TOOK MY PICTURE BEFORE I WAS READY!
I'M ON A TIGHT SCHEDULE, AMIGO!

BUT YOU DIDN'T EVEN GIVE ME A CHANCE TO SMILE!
OKAY, KID... I SHOULDN'T BE SUCH A SOFTIE, BUT OKAY.

I'LL GIVE YOU A DO-OVER. JUST SHOW ME A NICE SMILE... THAT'S GOOD... ANNND...

WHAT'S THE HOLD-UP HERE?
GAH!
KLIK!
Peirce

LISTEN, SHUTTERBUG, YOU WERE SUPPOSED TO BE **DONE** BY NOW!
SO SORRY, COACH!

JUST TRYING TO GET A **SMILE** OUT OF THIS YOUNG MAN!
WELL, THEN, GET **ON** WITH IT, KID!

JUST FLASH THOSE PEARLY WHITES AND LOOK **HAPPY**!

...LIKE **THIS**!
GOOD HEAVENS.
HOW 'BOUT I JUST USE LAST YEAR'S PICTURE?
Peirce

LET'S GET THIS DONE, FLASH, SO I CAN HAVE MY GYMNASIUM BACK!
OKAY, KID, BACK UP ON THE STOOL!

GOOD! OKAY, READY? A-ONE AND A-TWO AAANNNNND...

SMILE!
KLIK!

HOO! A LITTLE NIPPY TODAY! THIS IS PROBABLY THE LAST TIME I'LL PLAY THIS YEAR!
1ST TEE

...AND THIS IS THE LAST BALL IN MY BAG!

BUT THAT'S OKAY! A GOOD GOLFER DOESN'T **NEED** MORE THAN ONE BALL!

IF I CAN'T MAKE A BALL LAST FOR EIGHTEEN HOLES, I DON'T DESERVE TO PLAY GOLF! I'LL JUST GO HOME!

POW!

A DOZEN TOP-FLITES, PLEASE.
WHAT ABOUT THE WHOLE "GOING HOME" THING?

WHO ARE WE PLAYING TODAY?
ELMWOOD.

ARE THEY GOOD?
HA! THEY'RE **HORRIBLE**!
THEY HAVEN'T WON A GAME IN **FIVE YEARS**!

HA HA! WOULDN'T IT BE FUNNY IF...
DON'T SAY IT, CHAD.

...IF THEY ACTUALLY **BEAT** US?
DON'T SAY IT, CHAD!
Peirce

CHAD! WHAT ARE YOU DOING?
WHAT? WHAT DID I SAY?

YOU SAID ELMWOOD COULD BEAT US! YOU MIGHT HAVE JINXED US!

NOW WE HAVE TO COUNTERACT THAT JINX BEFORE WE TURN INTO LOSERS!

IT MAY BE TOO LATE!
...FOR ONE OF US, ANY-WAY.
WE'LL NEED A RABBIT'S FOOT, A 4-LEAF CLOVER, AND A BAG OF SKITTLES.

WOW. THESE GUYS LOOK **AWFUL**.
DOESN'T MATTER. CHAD JINXED US, SO WE'RE IN BIG TROUBLE.

REALLY.
YUP. JINXES TRUMP EVERY-THING. THEY TRUMP CHARMS, SPELLS, OMENS, CURSES... YOU NAME IT.

WHAT ABOUT DOOFS?
WHAT'S A DOOF?

DOOF!
Peirce

HALFTIME
GUYS, WE SHOULD BE WINNING THIS GAME **COMFORTABLY.** INSTEAD, IT'S **SCORELESS.**
COACH

WE'RE LETTING ELMWOOD DICTATE THE TEMPO! WE'RE LETTING THEM BEAT US TO THE BALL!
COACH

PLUS, WE'VE BEEN **JINXED** BY SOMEONE ON OUR TEAM WHO SHALL REMAIN NAMELESS!

RIGHT, **CHAD?**
I LOVE OUR TEAM SPIRIT.

CORNER KICK! MAN UP, GUYS! EVERYBODY COVER SOMEONE!

HERE IT COMES! I GOT THIS!

DOINK!

GOAL!
WHAT?
Peirce

REF! WAIT! NO GOAL! THAT WAS A **HAND BALL**!
NOPE. HE HEADED IT IN.

NO, IT WENT IN OFF HIS **HAND**! **ASK** HIM!
HEY, KID! DIDN'T THAT BALL GO IN OFF YOUR HAND?

I HAVE NO IDEA WHAT YOU'RE TALKING ABOUT.

WE'RE LOSING TO A TEAM THAT HASN'T WON A GAME IN FIVE YEARS.
WHAT-EVER HAPPENED TO THE HONOR SYSTEM?

TAP
TAP
TAP
TRICK OR TREATERS WELCOME

HI, DAD! WHAT'S IN THE BAG?
JUST SOME HALLOWEEN TREATS!

OOH! CANDY?
BETTER THAN CANDY!

COOKIES, THEN?
NO, THEY'RE NOT COOKIES, EXACTLY.

I FOUND THEM AT THE HEALTH FOOD STORE. THEY'RE... WELL, I'M NOT SURE WHAT YOU'D CALL 'EM...

THE IMPORTANT THING IS, THEY'RE SUGAR-FREE, GLUTEN-FREE, AND DAIRY-FREE! NO FAT, NO CALORIES!

TAP
TAP
TAP
DON'T BOTHER

I CAN'T BELIEVE WE'RE **LOSING** TO THESE GUYS!
HUDDLE UP, BOYS! HUDDLE UP!

LOOK, WE'RE BEHIND BY **ONE GOAL**! THAT'S **NOTHING**! WE CAN STILL WIN! IT'S TIME FOR SOME BOBCAT **PRIDE**!

BUT THERE'S ONLY EIGHTEEN SECONDS LEFT IN THE GAME.
EIGHTEEN SECONDS?

THEN STOP STANDING AROUND AND **SCORE**! **SCORE**! **SCORE**!!
GOODBYE BOBCAT PRIDE, HELLO BOBCAT PANIC.
peirce

BANG!
WE WON!

WE BEAT P.S. 38! WE WON! WE FINALLY WON!

OUR FIVE-YEAR LOSING STREAK IS OVER! WE WON!!

DO THEY HAVE TO BE SO OBNOXIOUS ABOUT IT?

COACH, WE'RE GOING TO PROTEST THIS GAME, RIGHT? THEY SCORED ON A **HAND BALL**!
NOT ACCORDING TO THE REF.

BUT THE REF WAS **WRONG**! TELL HIM HE SCREWED UP!
NATE, THE REFEREE'S WORD IS LAW! COACHES SHOULDN'T ARGUE WITH REFS.

... JUST LIKE **PLAYERS** SHOULDN'T ARGUE WITH **COACHES**.

THE HAND-SHAKE LINE IS THAT WAY.
SUBTLE.
COACH

GOOD GAME!
YEAH. SAME.
BUT TELL ME THE TRUTH: DO YOU **REALLY** THINK WINNING BY AN ILLEGAL GOAL IS A "GOOD GAME"?
DUDE, WHEN YOU'VE LOST SIXTY TIMES IN A ROW, WINNING BY AN ILLEGAL GOAL IS AN **AWESOME** GAME!
HE'S GOT A POINT!
YOU'RE NOT HELPING, CHAD.
Peirce

GETTING BEAT BY A TEAM THAT HAD LOST SIXTY GAMES IN A ROW. HOW HUMILIATING.
I'M NOT HUMILIATED!
2

I'M SORT OF **HAPPY** ABOUT IT, AREN'T YOU? I MEAN, THEY MADE **HISTORY**, AND **WE** WERE PART OF IT!

IT MAKES ME FEEL... FEEL...
2

...HUNGRY?
TOTALLY! MY PRE-GAME TWINKIE WORE OFF BY HALFTIME!
2
Peirce

DON'T TAKE IT SO HARD, NATE.
HOW CAN I **NOT** TAKE IT HARD?
ACH

THEY DIDN'T EVEN BEAT US FAIR AND SQUARE! THEY WON ON AN **ILLEGAL GOAL**!

YES, BUT THAT'S NOT WHY WE LOST. WHY DO **YOU** THINK WE LOST?
BECAUSE OUR OFFENSE **STUNK**.
COACH

...OR BECAUSE WE DIDN'T PLAY AS A **TEAM**.
YEAH, WHATEVER. BUT WE AGREE THAT IT WASN'T **MY** FAULT, RIGHT?
COACH
peirce

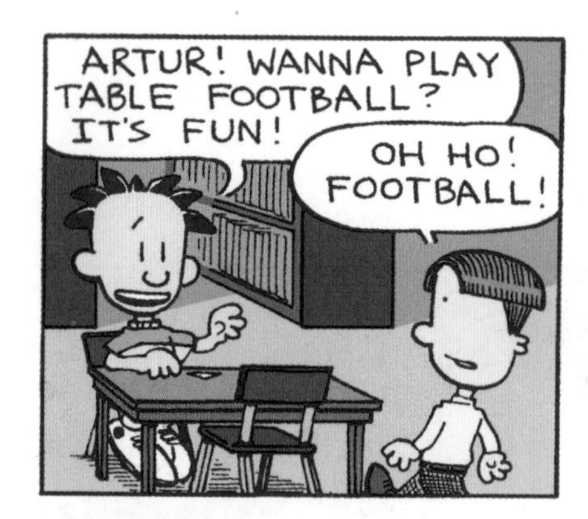
ARTUR! WANNA PLAY TABLE FOOTBALL? IT'S FUN!
OH HO! FOOTBALL!

...OR, AS YOU AMERICANS ARE CALL IT: SOCCER!
NO, NOT SOCCER! FOOT-BALL! USA STYLE!

HOKAY. SO OUTSIDE WE SHOULD GO, THEN.
NO, NO! WE PLAY RIGHT HERE!

BUT HOW WE PLAY WITH NO BALL?
WE'VE GOT A BALL! LOOK!

NATE. STOP JOKING. THAT IS A PAPER TRIANGLE ONLY.
NO DUH, ARTUR! IT'S A SUBSTITUTE BALL!

HA! BUT YOU CANNOT THROW OR KICK SUCH A BALL SO LITTLE AND POINTY!
WE DON'T THROW IT, ARTUR! WE DON'T KICK IT!

IT'S TABLE FOOTBALL! WE PLAY ON THE TABLE!
AH. HOKAY!

HIKES!
?
I CAN'T TAKE IT.

NATE, WHAT'S GOING ON HERE?
HM?

JUST...UH... Y'KNOW... JUST DOING MATH.

SEE?
THAT'S A TABLE FOOTBALL.

IT'S AN ISOSCELES TRIANGLE.
...WITH "CRUSH THE JETS" WRITTEN ON IT?
peirce

THAT'S ENOUGH, BOYS. LEAVE THE LIBRARY, PLEASE.
US? WHAT FOR?

PLAYING TABLE FOOTBALL.
WHAT? WAIT A MINUTE!

I'VE SEEN OTHER KIDS PLAYING THE EXACT SAME GAME, AND YOU DIDN'T THROW THEM OUT!

THOSE OTHER KIDS DIDN'T PAINT YARD LINES ON THE TABLE WITH "WITE-OUT."
THOSE WERE HERE WHEN WE SAT DOWN.

MRS. GODFREY, WE FINISHED READING CHAPTER FIVE! CAN WE PLAY TABLE FOOT-BALL?
WHAT? **NO!**

WHEN YOU FINISH **ONE** CHAPTER, YOU SHOULDN'T HAVE TO BE **TOLD** TO GO ON TO THE **NEXT** CHAPTER!

WOULD YOU RATHER **LEARN** SOMETHING OR WASTE YOUR TIME ON SOME SILLY **GAME**?

IS SHE SERIOUS?
WHY DOES SCHOOL ALWAYS HAVE TO BE ABOUT **LEARNING** STUFF?
PEIRCE

NATE! TEDDY! WHAT ARE YOU **DOING**?
PLAYING TABLE FOOTBALL!

YOU'RE **SUPPOSED** TO BE DOING THE **WORKSHEET** I GAVE YOU!
WE FINISHED THAT ALREADY!

THEN FOR HEAVEN'S SAKE, **HAND IT IN!**
OKAY...

JUST GIVE ME A SEC TO UNFOLD IT.
Peirce

AGAIN, NATE?
HI, MRS. CZERWICKI.

WHAT DID YOU DO THIS TIME?
I WAS PLAYING TABLE FOOTBALL IN CLASS.

I SEE. AND ARE YOU GOOD AT TABLE FOOTBALL?
ME? I'M THE BEST!

LATER...
THAT'S 49-14, ME!
HOW EMBARRASSING.
peirce

MY GOODNESS, NATE, WHY ARE YOU STILL HERE?
I HAD DETENTION.

DETENTION ONLY LASTS AN HOUR. IT'S ALMOST 6 P.M.!

MRS. CZERWICKI AND I WERE...UH... DOING SOMETHING, AND WE LOST TRACK OF TIME.
DOING WHAT?

WHO'S THE TABLE FOOTBALL CHAMP?
YOU ARE.
Peirce

WANNA RACE TO THE MAILBOX?
NO, THANKS.

HOW COME?
WHAT'S THE POINT? WE BOTH KNOW YOU'RE FASTER.

I'LL GIVE YOU A HEAD START!
NOPE.

I'LL RUN WITH MY HANDS IN MY POCKETS!
NO.
I'LL RUN BACKWARDS!
NUH-UH.

I'LL START FROM A SITTING POSITION!
HMM... OKAY.

...AND I'LL BE THE ONE TO SAY READY, SET, GO.
DEAL!

WHAT'S HAPPENING HERE?
I'M WINNING.
Peirce

I THINK IT STARTS AT 7:00.
SO LET'S MEET IN THE LOBBY AT 6:45.
WHAT'S UP, MEN?

OH... UH... WE WERE TALKING ABOUT GOING TO A MOVIE.
COOL! I'M IN!

YOU TELL HIM.
NO, **YOU** TELL HIM!
BUT YOU'LL EX-PLAIN IT BETTER!
ULP!
Peirce

HERE'S THE THING, NATE. WE'RE GOING TO THE MOVIE WITH PAIGE AND SHEILA.
THEY SORT OF WANT TO DOUBLE DATE.

SO IT MIGHT BE A LITTLE WEIRD IF YOU... I MEAN... Y'KNOW...
OH, SURE! I GET IT!

THAT'S OKAY, GUYS! NO PROBLEM! HA HA! I TOTALLY UNDER-STAND! HAVE A GREAT TIME! NO WORRIES!

NO WORRIES AT ALL.
Peirce

NATE, WHAT FOR YOU ARE LOOK SO SAD?
OH... FRANCIS AND TEDDY ARE GOING TO A MOVIE.

...AND THEY'RE BRINGING PAIGE AND SHEILA, SO IF I GO, I'LL JUST BE IN THE...
OH HO! SO THERE IS HAP-PENING A DOUBLE DATE!

THAT SOUNDS FUN TIMES! I WILL ASK FRANCIS AND TEDDY FOR ME AND JENNY TO GO, TOO!

WILL BE NOW A TRIPLE DATE!
OH, HOW I HATE HIM.

MR. ROSA, CAN I EAT LUNCH IN HERE?
SURE, NATE!

HOW'S YOUR LUNCH?
HORRIBLE.

...AND EVERYBODY WHO'S GOING TO THE MOVIE IS PART OF A COUPLE!
I SEE.

AND YOU'RE NOT PART OF A COUPLE?
SNORT! I SHOULD BE!

...AND IF JENNY EVER WAKES UP AND REALIZES WHAT A PINHEAD ARTUR IS, MAYBE I WILL BE PART OF A COUPLE!

THIS IS WHERE I RE-DIRECT HIM WITH CANDY.
OOH! SNO-CAPS!
Peirce

I KNOW TEDDY AND FRANCIS HAVE GIRL-FRIENDS, NATE, BUT THAT DOESN'T MEAN YOU HAVE TO!

YOU CAN BE SINGLE AND STILL LEAD A RICH, FULFILLING LIFE! I MEAN, LOOK AT ME!

OUCH.
YIKES.

COME ON, FRANCIS! RACE ME TO THE MAILBOX!
LISTEN, NATE: WHAT'S THE POINT OF A RACE? ANY RACE?

TO SEE WHO'S FASTER, RIGHT? BUT WE ALREADY KNOW WHO'S FASTER! YOU ARE!

SO THERE'S NO POINT IN RACING.
YES, THERE IS! JUST BECAUSE I'M FASTER DOESN'T MEAN I'LL WIN!

WHAT IF I GET A MUSCLE CRAMP? WHAT IF I TWIST MY ANKLE? THEN YOU COULD WIN!

THAT'S WHY PEOPLE RACE, FRANCIS! BECAUSE THE OUTCOME IS ALWAYS IN DOUBT! ANYTHING COULD HAPPEN!
HMM...

OKAY, YOU'RE ON!
NOW YOU'RE TALKIN'! READY... SET...

DOOF!

ZIP!

"ANYTHING COULD HAPPEN"!

SO LONG, DAD. I'M GOING TO THE MOVIES.
BUT I THOUGHT YOUR FRIENDS MADE IT A "COUPLES ONLY" THING.
SPORTS

THEY DID.
SO HOW COME YOU'RE GOING? TRYING TO CRASH THEIR PARTY?

WHAT? **NO!** I'M A **FILM BUFF**, THAT'S ALL! THERE HAPPENS TO BE A MOVIE PLAYING THAT I REALLY, REALLY WANT TO SEE!
WHAT MOVIE?

UMMM... IT'S... UH... THE TITLE IS... YOU'VE PROBABLY NEVER HEARD OF... UH... IT'S NOT COMING TO MIND RIGHT NOW...
SOUNDS FASCINATING.
peirce

THERE THEY ARE! ALL PAIRED UP FOR THEIR BIG ROMANTIC MOVIE NIGHT!
NOW SHO

FINE! LET 'EM! I DON'T NEED TO DO WHAT THEY'RE DOING!

I DON'T NEED TO BE PART OF A COUPLE TO HAVE FUN!
OON
NO

LOTS OF PEOPLE GO TO MOVIES ALONE!
YES, I KNOW I'M EARLY! THAT'S THE POINT!
TICKET
Peirce

SCHOOL PICTURE GUY!
AH! WHAT'S SHAKIN', KID? WHAT'S NEW?

JUST GOING TO A MOVIE. BY MY-SELF.
HM. I HEAR YOU, AMIGO. I, TOO, AM FLYING SOLO THIS EVENING.

I WAS TURNED DOWN COLD BY THE LADY I HAD HOPED WOULD BE MY COMPANION FOR TONIGHT'S PROCEEDINGS!

YOUR MOM?
INDEED. EVIDENTLY I CAN'T COMPETE WITH "JUDGE JUDY."

...AND THE CINEMATOGRAPHY IS...
SIR? THIS IS A NON-SMOKING BUILDING.

I'M NOT SMOKING, YOUNG MAN! THIS PIPE IS MERELY A PROP TO LEND REALISM TO MY COSTUME!

CHUCKLE! AND IT OBVIOUSLY WORKED, SINCE YOU MISTOOK ME FOR AN ACTUAL WIZARD!

KID, TELL HIM I'M NOT A WIZARD.
YEAH. NOT EVEN CLOSE.
Peirce

I GOTTA GET IN THERE. THE MOVIE'S ABOUT TO START.
HAPPY TRAILS, KID!

HOLY **COW**! IT'S **PACKED**!
YUP. THERE'S A SEAT OVER THERE.
XIT

GREAT. NOW I HAVE TO SIT NEXT TO SOMEBODY I DON'T EVEN...
POP

NO!
GAH!

GINA! WHAT ARE YOU DOING HERE?
WHAT DO YOU THINK, PINHEAD? WATCHING A MOVIE!

WELL, I DON'T WANT YOU SITTING NEXT TO ME!
THEN MOVE YOUR BUTT, BRAINLESS! I WAS HERE FIRST!

I CAN'T MOVE! THIS IS THE ONLY SEAT LEFT!
WHAT DO YOU EXPECT ME TO DO ABOUT IT?

SHUT UP, LOVEBIRDS! THE MOVIE'S STARTING!
LOVE-BIRDS?!

THIS BOOK ABOUT EVOLUTION IS **FASCINATING!**

WHAT **IS** EVOLUTION?
IT'S THE WAY SPECIES CHANGE IN RESPONSE TO THEIR ENVIRONMENT!

ALL SPECIES ARE EVOLVING, **ALL** THE TIME!
EVEN **US**?

SURE! LET'S SAY THAT TOMORROW, THERE'S ANOTHER **ICE AGE!**

PEOPLE WOULD PROBABLY BECOME **HAIRIER** TO PROTECT THEMSELVES FROM THE COLD!

HA! THAT'S FUNNY!
SO... WE'D ALL JUST START GROWING MORE HAIR?
NO, NO...

IT WOULD HAPPEN **GRADUALLY!** IT WOULD TAKE **THOUSANDS OF YEARS!**

TOUGH LUCK, DAD!
PAT PAT!
THANKS SO MUCH.
Peirce

I CAN'T BELIEVE THE ONLY SEAT LEFT IS NEXT TO **YOU**.
WELL, THEN, WHY DON'T YOU **LEAVE**?

WHY DON'T **YOU**, GINA?
BECAUSE I PAID FIVE DOLLARS FOR A TICKET, AND I INTEND TO GET MY MONEY'S WORTH!

FIVE BUCKS? WAIT A MINUTE, **MY** TICKET COST **EIGHT**! HOW COME YOU ONLY HAD TO PAY **FIVE**?

I SHOWED THEM MY REPORT CARD AND THEY GAVE ME A "GOOD STUDENT" DISCOUNT!
GAG ME.

I'M GOING FOR SOME POPCORN.
HERE, GET ME SOME WHILE YOU'RE AT IT.

WHAT? EXCUSE ME, GINA, BUT I DON'T REMEMBER OFFERING TO BE YOUR ERRAND BOY!

JUST GET HER THE POPCORN, KID. IT'LL BE EASIER THAT WAY.

WHAT'S THAT SUPPOSED TO MEAN?
NOTHING, DEAR.
NO BUTTER, LIGHT SALT.

FRANCIS! THERE'S NATE!
NATE!

WHAT ARE YOU DOING HERE?
ME?... OH... UH... Y'KNOW, WATCHING THE MOVIE... BUYING SOME POPCORN...

SOME POPCORN IS RIGHT! HOW COME YOU'RE BUYING TWO?
WAIT, ARE YOU HERE WITH SOMEBODY?
WHAT? NO, I...

WHAT'S TAKING YOU SO LONG?
GAH!

NATE! YOU AND GINA ARE ON A **DATE**?
ARE YOU **INSANE**, FRANCIS? OF **COURSE** NOT!

THE SEAT NEXT TO HER WAS THE ONLY ONE **LEFT!** TELL THEM, GINA! TELL THEM WE'RE NOT ON A DATE!

TELL THEM, GINA.
Peirce

TELL THEM, GINA!
OOOOOH!

WOOO! NATE AND GINA! HEH HEH!
GINA! COME ON!

TELL THESE CLOWNS THAT YOU AND I AREN'T ON A DATE!
THEY KNOW WE'RE NOT ON A DATE, YOU IDIOT!

EVERYBODY KNOWS I'D NEVER DATE A HALF-WIT LIKE YOU!
AH-HA! HEAR THAT, GUYS? EVERYBODY KNOWS...

SHE CALLED YOU HALF-WIT!
THAT'S SO ROMANTIC!
WAIT, WHAT?

HI, NATE! HOW WAS THE MOVIE?
OKAY.

SEE ANYBODY YOU KNEW THERE?
WHAT? WHO, ME? WHY ARE YOU ASKING **THAT**?

WHAT DID YOU HEAR? DID SOMEBODY TELL YOU SOMETHING? WHY ARE YOU GRILLING ME ABOUT SOME STUPID MOVIE?
Peirce

I LOVE THESE FATHER-SON CHATS.
... BECAUSE I'M NOT GINA'S LOVE MONKEY! I'M **NOT**!

PREPARE TO BE **CRUSHED**, SCRUB! YOU GUYS HAVE NO **CHANCE**!

WE'VE GOT BETTER PLAYERS... A SMARTER COACH...

EVEN OUR **CHEERLEADERS** ARE CUTER!
OH, I DON'T KNOW ABOUT THAT.

SOME OF OUR CHEERLEADERS ARE PRETTY CUTE.
LIKE THAT TALL ONE WITH THE PONYTAIL.

AND YOU KNOW WHAT? I THINK SHE MIGHT HAVE A LITTLE **CRUSH** ON YOU!
HUH?

CHECK IT OUT! SHE'S LOOKING AT YOU!
SHE **IS**?

ZIP!
! !

SWISH!

MY MISTAKE. SHE WAS LOOKING AT ME.
Peirce

DAD, I'D LIKE TO CALL YOUR ATTENTION TO TWO IMPORTANT FACTS.

FACT 1: I WANT A DOG FOR CHRISTMAS. FACT 2: YOU'RE ON A DIET.

IF YOU GET ME A DOG, I WILL RE-CONSIDER MY PLAN TO CREATE AN AMUSING WEB PAGE ABOUT YOUR DIETARY MIS-ADVENTURES.

'TWAS THE BRIBE BEFORE CHRISTMAS.
DAY ONE: CLOSE ENCOUNTER WITH A "KFC DOUBLE DOWN."
Peirce

DAD, ISN'T THERE AN EXPRESSION THAT SAYS, "EVERY-THING IS NEGOTIABLE"?
I GUESS SO.
SPORTS

SO LET'S NEGOTIATE! WHAT DO I HAVE TO DO SO THAT YOU'LL GET ME A DOG?

YOU HAVE TO ACCEPT THE FACT THAT I WON'T GET YOU A DOG.
SPORTS

THAT MAKES NO SENSE.
NEITHER DOES NEGOTIATING WITH A SIXTH GRADER.
SPORTS
Peirce

WHAT A NICE DAY! I THINK I'LL GO OUTSIDE AND PLAY WITH MY DOG!

OH **WAIT**, I FOR**GOT**! I DON'T **HAVE** A DOG!
THUNK!

I GUESS I'LL JUST STAY INSIDE AND PLAY WITH THIS **SOCK PUPPET**!
CITY

PRETTY SAD, RIGHT?
I WAS JUST THINKING THAT.
CITY
Peirce

DAD, IT'S UP TO **ME** WHAT TO GIVE YOU AND ELLEN FOR CHRISTMAS, RIGHT?
RIGHT.
METRO

YOU MAY GIVE YOUR SISTER AND ME ANYTHING YOU LIKE.

...EXCEPT A DOG.
METRO

ANOTHER BRILLIANT PLAN FOILED.
BY THE WAY, I COULD USE A NEW BELT.

ONCE AGAIN MY DAD IS REFUSING TO GET ME A DOG FOR CHRISTMAS.
MAYBE YOU'RE SETTING YOUR SIGHTS TOO HIGH.

TRY ASKING HIM FOR A HAMSTER OR SOMETHING.
A **HAMSTER**? FRANCIS, A HAMSTER ISN'T ANYTHING LIKE A **DOG**!

HNK! HACK! HOCH HOCCH!

RRRETCH!
THAT MIGHT BE A GOOD THING!
SPITSY, THAT'S DISGUSTING.
Peirce

WELL, SPITSY, LOOKS LIKE I WON'T BE GETTING A DOG FOR CHRISTMAS... AGAIN.

BUT AT LEAST I CAN STILL PLAY WITH YOU, RIGHT?... FETCH!
ZING!

FETCH.

OH, BROTHER.
Z
PEIRCE

IF I HIT THAT TREE WITH THIS SNOWBALL, IT MEANS...
NOT **THIS** AGAIN.

NOT WHAT AGAIN?
YOU'RE ALWAYS ASSIGNING **MEANING** TO RANDOM ACTS OF SKILL!

"IF I HIT THAT TREE, IT MEANS JENNY LIKES ME!"
"IF I MAKE THIS SHOT, IT MEANS I'M GOING TO BE RICH!"
IT'S **RIDIC-ULOUS**!

IF YOU HIT THAT TREE WITH THAT SNOWBALL, NATE, YOU KNOW WHAT IT MEANS? **NOTHING**!

WHAT IF I HIT SOMETHING ELSE?
IT DOESN'T MATTER **WHAT** YOU HIT! IT HAS NO MEANING! **NONE**!

POW!

YOU'RE **RIGHT**! I FEEL SO **EMPTY**!

HO, HO, **HO**!
GRAM! GRAMPS!

MERRY CHRISTMAS, CHAMP!
ELLEN! HI, HONEY!

ARE YOU STILL DATING THAT NICE GORDIE?
YES, GRAM!

AT LEAST **SOME**BODY IN THIS FAMILY HAS A SOCIAL LIFE.
I'M WORKING ON IT, MOM.
Peirce

COOL! A SWISS ARMY KNIFE!
YUP! THAT'S THE GENUINE ARTICLE, M'BOY!

IT'S GOT A MINI SAW, A SCREWDRIVER, A SCISSORS... WHATEVER YOU MIGHT NEED IN ANY EMERGENCY!
ANY EMERGENCY?

WHAT IF YOU STAB YOURSELF IN THE LEG WHILE DEMON-STRATING YOUR SWISS ARMY KNIFE TO A CUB SCOUT TROOP?

THAT WAS A FREAK ACCIDENT, MARGE.
THOSE POOR BOYS WERE TRAUMA-TIZED!
Peirce

MERCY! LOOKS LIKE SOMEBODY GOT EVERYTHING ON HIS WISH LIST!
YEAH... **ALMOST.**

ALMOST?
I ASK FOR A DOG EVERY YEAR, BUT I NEVER GET ONE.

FOR HEAVEN'S SAKE, MARTY, IF THE BOY WANTS A DOG, GIVE HIM A DOG!
!

GRAMPS! MY MAN!
DAD, CAN I SPEAK TO YOU IN THE KITCHEN?

CHEER UP, SWEETIE! MAYBE YOUR DAD WILL LET YOU GET A DOG **NEXT** CHRISTMAS!
I DOUBT IT.

HE THINKS PET-SITTING FOR SPITSY IS GOOD ENOUGH.
WHO'S SPITSY?

ACORN ST.
WHIMPER!

OH, DEAR.
AGAIN?

GRAMPS, DO YOU REMEMBER THE FIRST CHRISTMAS GIFT GRAM EVER GAVE YOU?
I SURE DO, ELLEN!

SHE GAVE ME THIS BEAUTIFUL POCKET WATCH WITH OUR INITIALS ENGRAVED ON THE BACK!

AND GRAM, WHAT DID GRAMPS GIVE **Y**-
A VACUUM CLEANER.

...WHICH **STILL WORKS**, BY THE WAY!
HOW WOULD **YOU** KNOW?
peirce

YOU KNOW, MARGE, SEEING ELLEN AND HER BEAU MAKES ME THINK ABOUT WHEN **WE** WERE HIGH SCHOOL SWEETHEARTS!

CHUCKLE! REMEMBER WHEN I KISSED YOU UNDER THE MISTLETOE AT THE "HOLIDAY HIJINKS" DANCE?
WINK!

THAT WASN'T ME. THAT WAS THAT TRAMP ABIGAIL OSTRANG.

KOFF! ...WHICH IS WHY I DON'T REMEMBER IT **EITHER**!
I WAS BEHIND THE BLEACHERS WITH ARNIE PFEIFFER!

OW!

DAD! I GOT A SLIVER IN MY FOOT!
hop hop

CAN YOU GET IT OUT?
I CAN'T EVEN **SEE** IT.
WHAT'S UP?

I'VE GOT A SLIVER, GRAMPS.
IS THIS IT? DOWN NEAR THE HEEL?
THAT'S JUST DIRT.

IT'S UP NEAR MY BIG TOE.
CAN YOU SEE ANYTHING, DAD?
NOT A DARN THING.

OW! **OW!** THAT'S IT!
OOH. THAT'S REALLY **IN** THERE.
MM. THAT'S DEEP.

MAYBE IT JUST HAS TO WORK ITSELF OUT.
YUP. YUP.
OH, FOR HEAVEN'S SAKE. STEP ASIDE.

THERE. IT'S OUT.
ZWINK!

FASTEST TWEEZERS IN THE WEST!
EXCEPT WHEN I ASK HER TO PLUCK MY EAR HAIR.

AH, OUR ANNUAL NEW YEAR'S EVE MONOPOLY GAME!
LET'S TAKE A "NO CHEATING" PLEDGE.

WAIT, ARE WE MISS-ING ONE OF THE DICE?
LIKE, WE ALL THREE PROMISE NOT TO CHEAT DURING THE GAME.

AH, **HERE** IT IS!
JUST SO... Y'KNOW... THE GAME'S FAIR AND EVERYONE HAS AN EQUAL CHANCE TO WIN.

ROLL TO SEE WHO GOES FIRST!
HE'S NOT LISTENING.
I WON-DER WHY.

HEY! THE TOP HAT'S MISSING!
SO?

THE TOP HAT'S MY LUCKY PIECE, TEDDY! I'M ALWAYS THE TOP HAT! IT'S TRADITION!
OH, BROTHER.

WHO CARES WHAT PIECE YOU ARE? IF THE TOP HAT'S NOT THERE, PICK ANOTHER PIECE!
OKAY, OKAY...

BUT I WANT IT NOTED THAT I'M OFFICIALLY PLAYING THIS GAME UNDER PROTEST.
I THINK WE ALL ARE.
peirce

JUST PICK A PIECE, ALREADY!
DON'T RUSH ME, FRANCIS! I HAVE TO FIND ONE WITH GOOD LUCK VIBES!
F

AH! MAYBE THE THIMBLE WILL BE AN ACCEPTABLE SUBSTITUTE FOR MY LUCKY TOP HAT!

THIMBLE THIMBLE THIMBLE THIMBLE THIMMMMMMMMMM MMMMMMMMBLE. MMMMMMMMM...
F

NOPE. NOT FEELIN' IT.
IS IT JUST ME, OR WAS THAT KIND OF CREEPY?
F
Peirce

PARK PLACE! I'LL BUY IT!
WHAT? WAIT A MINUTE!

TWO TURNS AGO, YOU DIDN'T EVEN HAVE ENOUGH MONEY TO BUY A RAILROAD! YOU WERE BROKE!

AND NOW YOU'RE RICH ENOUGH TO BUY ONE OF THE MOST EXPENSIVE PROPERTIES ON THE BOARD? HOW?

I SAVE FAST.
THIS IS WHY PEOPLE HATE BANKERS.
Peirce

YOU'RE ACCUSING ME OF CHEATING, FRANCIS? **ME** ?
WELL, LET'S SEE...

YOU SPENT BOTH OF THE $500 BILLS YOU HAD AT THE START OF THE GAME... AND NOW, **MAGICALLY,** YOU HAVE **ANOTHER** $ 500 BILL!

WHAT WOULD **YOU** CALL IT?

SAVVY INVEST-ING.
TOLD YOU WE SHOULD'VE PLAYED JENGA.
Peirce

5...6...7... **RATS!** THAT'S THE THIRD TIME IN A ROW I'VE LANDED ON A HOTEL!

WELL, THAT DOES IT! I'M BROKE! BUSTED! LOOKS LIKE YOU WIN, FRANCIS!

GOOD JOB.

THAT'S MORE LIKE IT.
THE GAME GOT MORE FUN WHEN WE ADDED A REFEREE!

HEY, SOMETHING JUST FELL OUT OF KATY'S NOTEBOOK!

KATY, YOU DROPPED... MMPH!
SSHH, TEDDY!

WHAT'S YOUR PROBLEM?
CHECK THIS OUT!

IT'S ONE OF THOSE NOTES KATY AND CLAIRE ARE ALWAYS PASSING BACK AND FORTH DURING CLASS!

SO?
SO, HAVEN'T YOU EVER WONDERED WHAT THEY'RE SAYING TO EACH OTHER?

WELL...
OF COURSE YOU HAVE! NOW'S OUR CHANCE TO SEE WHAT'S SO IMPORTANT!
FLIP
FLIP

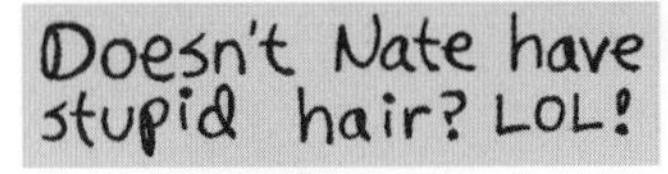
Doesn't Nate have stupid hair? LOL!

RIP
RIP
RIP
RIP
RIP
RIP
RIP

THIS TEAM WE'RE PLAYING TODAY IS UNDEFEATED.
YEAH, BECAUSE THEY'VE GOT DEVON KENDALL.

WHO'S DEVON KENDALL?
ONLY THE BEST PLAYER IN THE **STATE**! HE'S ALREADY BEING SCOUTED BY **COLLEGES**!

SO THERE MIGHT BE **SCOUTS** AT THE GAME?

I SHOULDN'T HAVE SAID THAT.
NO KID-DING.
HELLO, **SCHOLAR-SHIP**!
Peirce

COACH, I HEAR THESE GUYS HAVE A SUPER-STAR ON THEIR ROSTER!
YUP. DEVON KENDALL.

LET ME GUARD HIM, COACH! I'LL SHOW HIM DEFENSE LIKE HE'S NEVER SEEN! I'LL GET IN HIS KITCHEN AND SHUT HIM DOWN!

NOW... LET ME AT 'IM! WHICH ONE IS HE?
RIGHT THERE.

THE ONE WHO JUST DID A REVERSE TWO-HAND TOMAHAWK JAM.
YOU KNOW, MAYBE WE SHOULD DOUBLE-TEAM THIS GUY.
Peirce

SO! YOU'RE DEVON KENDALL! HEY, I HEAR YOU'RE A POINT GUARD! SO AM I!

I GUESS YOU AND I ARE SORT OF ALIKE!

ARE YOU AVERAGING 45 POINTS, 14 ASSISTS, AND 12 REBOUNDS PER GAME?

OUR WHOLE TEAM ISN'T AVERAGING THAT.
WELL, EXCUSE ME FOR NOT BEING JOE STATS!
Peirce

OKAY, SO THIS KID'S **SUPPOSEDLY** THE FASTEST PLAYER IN THE LEAGUE.

WELL, WE'LL JUST **SEE** HOW FAST HE...

! ? !

HEY, YOUR GUY JUST SCORED.
THANKS.
CATS
2
Peirce

THIS KID'S AWESOME! I CAN'T SLOW HIM DOWN!
TRY TO GET UNDER HIS SKIN WITH SOME OF YOUR FAMOUS TRASH TALK.

YEAH! GOOD IDEA, TEDDY!

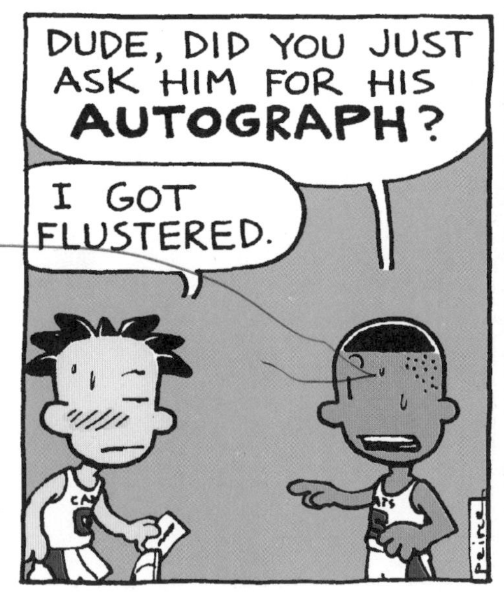
DUDE, DID YOU JUST ASK HIM FOR HIS AUTOGRAPH?
I GOT FLUSTERED.

MAN! THOSE GUYS **CRUSHED** US.
YEAH, THANKS TO DEVON KENDALL.

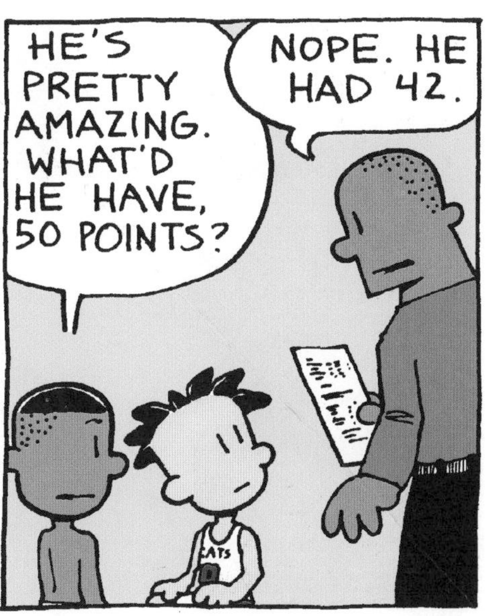
HE'S PRETTY AMAZING. WHAT'D HE HAVE, 50 POINTS?
NOPE. HE HAD 42.
CATS

NATE, YOU ACTUALLY HELD HIM TO THREE POINTS **UNDER** HIS SEASON AVERAGE.

SO YOU WERE SLIGHTLY LESS PATHETIC THAN EVERYONE **ELSE** HE'S PLAYED!
YES!
CATS
Peirce

WHEW!
PRETTY HEAVY STUFF, EH DAD?

DAD?

DAD!

DAD! ARE YOU OKAY? ARE YOU DIZZY? ARE YOU HAVING CHEST PAINS?
CHEST PAINS?

I'M MAKING A SNOW ANGEL, YOU KNUCKLE-HEAD!

A SNOW ANGEL! HA HA! OKAY! FALSE ALARM! WHAT A RELIEF!
DIZZY! CHEST PAINS! *SNORT!* PLEASE!

HOW HELPLESS DOES HE THINK I AM?

WANT SOME HELP GETTING UP?
YUP.

OH. HEY, ARTUR.
NATE. I AM NEED YOUR HELP WITH A PROBLEM, PLEASE.

I'M A LITTLE BUSY RIGHT NOW.
BUT IT IS AN **EMERGENCY,** THIS PROBLEM!

I AM WORRY THAT BETWEEN JENNY AND ME, THINGS ARE NOT SO GOOD.

TELL ME EVERY-THING!
AH-HA! I **KNEW** YOU WOULD BE TO HELPING!
Peirce

SO, ARTUR: TELL ME ABOUT THESE PROBLEMS BETWEEN YOU AND JENNY.
YES. IT IS HUGE BUMMER.

LATELY IS SO **DIFFERENT** SHE IS ACTING. LIKE SHE IS NOT ANYMORE **HAPPY** WITH ME.

I AM SURE SHE SOON WILL TO BREAK UP WITH ME.
REALLY? THAT'S **GREAT**!

...LY DISTRESSING. **GREATLY** DISTRESSING.
THANK YOU, NATE. YOU ARE TOTAL PAL.
Peirce

WHAT'S UP, BOYS?
I THINK JENNY IS WANT TO BREAK UP WITH ME.

WHAT? BUT YOU GUYS ARE A GREAT COUPLE!
YES, THIS ALSO IS WHAT I THINK. BUT SHE MAYBE DOES NOT THINK IT.

SO I AM ASK NATE FOR HELP, BECAUSE HE IS EXPERT AT TALKING TO GIRLS!

HEH HEH!
UH... YOU KNOW WHAT "EXPERT" MEANS, RIGHT?
DON'T LISTEN TO THEM, ARTUR.
Peirce

SO YOU WILL TALK TO JENNY, HOKAY? TO FIND OUT WHY SHE IS ACT DIFFERENT LATELY.
SURE, ARTUR.

AH! THANK YOU, NATE! I KNEW THAT YOU WOULD BE FOR THIS JOB THE BEST PERSON!

BECAUSE YOU HAVE **KNOW** HER FOR SINCE YOU WERE **BABIES**, RIGHT?
RIGHT.

REMEMBER HOW YOU THOUGHT YOU WERE CRAZY IN LOVE WITH HER?
OH, HOW I HATE HIM.
Peirce

ARTUR WANTS YOU TO TALK TO JENNY FOR HIM? **YOU**?
NATURALLY! I'M THE IDEAL TROUBLESHOOTER!

RIIIIIIGHT.
I KNOW WHAT YOU'RE THINKING, FRANCIS, BUT I'M **OVER** JENNY! MY CRUSH ON HER IS **HISTORY**!

MY ONLY GOAL IS TO HELP ARTUR AND JENNY GET THEIR ROMANCE BACK ON TRACK!

HI, THERE.
Peirce

JENNY, M'LADY! WHAT'S NEW?
WHAT DO **YOU** CARE?

JUST WONDERING HOW EVERYTHING'S GOING BETWEEN YOU AND ARTUR, THAT'S ALL!

SNIFF!

WAAAAH!
YIKES.

THAT'S GREAT! I'LL TELL HIM!

AWESOME NEWS, MATT! SHE LIKES YOU!
SHE DOES?

YUP! WHEN I TOLD HER "MATT'S GOT A HUGE CRUSH ON YOU," SHE WAS TOTALLY STOKED!

THEN SHE SAID: "ASK HIM IF HE WANTS TO GO TO THE DANCE WITH ME"!
WOW! I SURE DO!

WELL, THEN, I GUESS IT'S OFFICIAL! MATT AND ANNA ARE THE SCHOOL'S HOT NEW COUPLE!
ANNA?

I ASKED YOU TO TALK TO HANNAH!

OHHHH.

HI AGAIN.
IT'S HARD TO FIND GOOD HELP NOWADAYS.

JENNY, CHILLAX! ALL I DID WAS ASK ABOUT YOU AND ARTUR!
SNIFF!

ARE YOU GUYS... AHEM!... ON THE OUTS, MAYBE?
NO.

THEN WHAT'S THE MATTER?

!
I'M MOVING.

JENNY! YOU... YOU'RE MOVING?
TO SEATTLE.

MY MOM'S COMPANY HAS AN OFFICE IN SEATTLE, AND THAT'S WHERE THEY'RE SENDING HER.

BUT... SEATTLE IS, LIKE, THREE THOUSAND MILES AWAY!
I KNOW.

THREE THOUSAND MILES AWAY FROM ME!
YOU'RE NOT HELPING.

I'LL NEVER GO TO HIGH SCHOOL WITH MY FRIENDS... OR GO TO A PROM... OR GRADUATE, OR...OR...

...AND YOU'LL NEVER FIND OUT THAT **ONE** OF THOSE FRIENDS WHO'S RIGHT UNDER YOUR **NOSE** HAS ACTUALLY BEEN YOUR PERFECT **SOUL MATE** THE WHOLE TIME!

LAST MONTH, MY MOM TOLD ME THERE WAS A 50% CHANCE WE'D HAVE TO MOVE TO SEATTLE.

THEN LAST WEEK, SHE TOLD ME IT WAS MORE LIKE 80%.

THEN YESTERDAY, SHE SAID IT WAS 100%.
SNIFF!

100% NEVER SOUNDED SO BAD.

I TALKED TO JENNY FOR YOU, ARTUR. THE GOOD NEWS IS: SHE STILL LIKES YOU.

THE BAD NEWS IS: SHE'S MOVING TO SEATTLE AND YOU'LL PROBABLY NEVER SEE HER AGAIN.

ZOW!

WAY TO BREAK IT TO HIM GENTLY.
WELL, WHY SHOULD I BE THE ONLY ONE WHO FEELS LOUSY?
Peirce

I CAN'T BELIEVE JENNY'S **MOVING**!
YEAH. POOR ARTUR.
POOR **ARTUR**?

YES, POOR ARTUR! HE'S HER **BOY-FRIEND**!
HE'S HER **CURRENT** BOYFRIEND!

BUT AS HER FUTURE BOYFRIEND OF DESTINY, **I'M** SUFFERING A LOT MORE THAN **HE** IS!

DID HE JUST CALL HIMSELF A FUTURE BOYFRIEND OF DESTINY?
I'VE STOPPED LISTENING.
YAK YAK YA
YAK YAK YAK
YAK YAK Y
YAK
Peirce

HA HA HA
OW! HA HA
SCRUB
SCRUB SCRUB
GUYS! STOP! WHY YOU ARE FIGHTING?

WE'RE JUST GOOFING AROUND, ARTUR!
YEAH, THAT'S WHAT GUYS DO!

SO YOU ARE PALS STILL, THEN?
OW!...OF COURSE!
SCRUB SCRUB
WHAT'S A LITTLE NOOGIE BETWEEN FRIENDS?

...OR A LITTLE FLICK TO THE EAR?
RIGHT!
THWIT!

... OR A LITTLE SLAP ON THE BACK!
OW!
SMAK!

...OR A LITTLE PUNCH IN THE ARM!
HEY!
POW!

KNOCK IT OFF!

JUST SO YOU KNOW: THEY ARE NOT FOR REAL FIGHTING!

OKAY, THIS IS GETTING TO BE A BIT MUCH.
WHAT IS?

ARTUR AND JENNY! WE ALL KNOW THEY'RE GOING TO MISS EACH OTHER, BUT... I MEAN, ENOUGH ALREADY!

THEY'VE BEEN HUG-GING FOR, LIKE, TWO HOURS! CAN'T THEY GIVE IT A REST?

HOW ABOUT JUST A BASIC FIST BUMP?
OKAY. HOLD STILL.
Peirce

I CANNOT BELIEVE TO **SEATTLE** YOU ARE MOVING!
NEITHER CAN I!

I AM GOING TO MISS YOU!
I'LL MISS YOU, TOO! SEATTLE IS SO FAR **AWAY!**

...BUT NOT FAR ENOUGH.
MOVE, ARTUR. I'M CUTTIN' IN.
PEIRCE

HERE'S MY MASTER PLAN: JENNY MOVES TO SEATTLE, OKAY, BUT SHE AND I STAY IN **VERY** CLOSE CONTACT!

THEN, SIX YEARS FROM NOW, WE BOTH GET ACCEPTED AT THE VERY SAME COLLEGE!

WHEN SHE SEES ME ON CAMPUS DURING FRESHMAN ORIENT-ATION, SHE REALIZES SHE'S BEEN MADLY IN LOVE WITH ME THE WHOLE TIME!

THEN, TRAGICALLY, YOU FLUNK OUT AFTER TWO WEEKS!
AND SHE ELOPES WITH A HUNKY ECON MAJOR!

JENNY, ALL YOUR CLASSMATES MADE CARDS TO WISH YOU GOOD LUCK IN SEATTLE!
THEY **DID**?

WOW! THESE ARE SO **NICE**!
THEY'RE SO **SWEET**!
THEY'RE SO...

ONLY IF WE WERE THE LAST TWO HUMANS ON THE FACE OF THE EARTH.
SO IT **COULD** HAPPEN!
Peirce

SEATTLE BEFORE
JENNY?
JENNY, I STILL CAN'T
JENNY? COULD I SPEAK TO YOU FOR A SEC?

I... UH... I KNOW I'M PROBABLY A TOTAL PAIN SOMETIMES, BUT... I JUST WANT TO SAY... Y'KNOW...

OH, YOU'RE NOT A TOTAL PAIN, NATE.
I'M **NOT**?

GUYS! I'M NOT A TOTAL PAIN!
THE JURY'S STILL OUT ON THAT ONE.
Peirce

I HAVE TO GO. ARTUR'S WALKING ME HOME, AND THEN I HAVE TO FINISH PACKING.
OH. OKAY.

WELL... BYE, JENNY.
BYE, NATE.

Peirce

YOU GUYS READY TO TAKE A BREAK? I'VE GOT DONUTS!
WOW!
SURE! THANKS, DAD!
SUPA-SNO

MMM! THEY'RE WARM!
SNIFFA SNIFFA SNUFFA SNIFFA
SPITSY, NO!

THESE ARE FOR ME AND CHAD, NOT YOU!

FIND YOUR OWN FOOD!
!

CHOMPF!
HSSSSSSSSSSSSS

BAD, BAD, BAD, BAD, BAD, BAD, BAD, BAD, BAD, BAD, BAD, BAD DOG.
Peirce

I CANNOT BELIEVING JENNY IS GONE TO SEATTLE.
I MISS HER SO MUCH.

PAT PAT

PAT PAT

WHACK!
WHACK!
WHACK!
WHACK!

JENNY'S GONE, BUT BELIEVE ME, SHE AND I WILL KEEP IN TOUCH!

SHE GAVE ME HER CELL PHONE NUMBER BEFORE SHE LEFT! IN FACT, I THINK I'LL CALL HER RIGHT **NOW**!
beep
boop
beep
boop
boop

YYYYELLO, IS JENNY THERE?
JENNY.
WHAT?

NO, I'M NOT MAKING AN APPOINTMENT FOR AN **OIL CHANGE**!
HOW ROMANTIC!
Peirce

MR. ROSA, I'VE RECENTLY EXPERIENCED A MAJOR TRAGEDY IN MY PERSONAL LIFE.

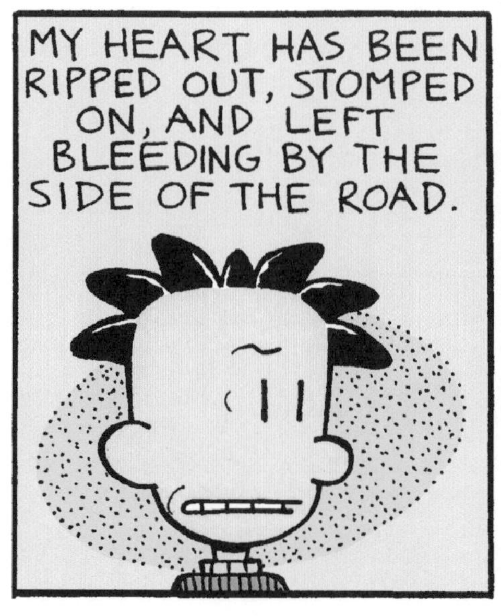
MY HEART HAS BEEN RIPPED OUT, STOMPED ON, AND LEFT BLEEDING BY THE SIDE OF THE ROAD.

I WANT TO USE TODAY'S CLASS TO DEAL WITH MY PAIN AND ANGUISH THROUGH THE POWER OF **ART**!

GOT ANY PIPE CLEANERS?
THIRD SHOEBOX ON THE LEFT.
Peirce

USUALLY, ART MAKES ME FEEL BETTER WHEN SOMETHING'S BOTHERING ME, BUT NOT TODAY.

LET ME TRY ONE MORE THING. THIS PRETTY MUCH **ALWAYS** WORKS.
SLOSH
SLOSH

FWING!
Peirce

HEY!
THERE WE GO!
EVEN I FEEL BETTER!

I'VE POURED EVERY OUNCE OF MYSELF INTO THIS PAINTING. I'VE GIVEN IT EVERY-THING I HAVE.

I'M PHYSICALLY AND EMOTIONALLY SPENT.

AND NOW... I MUST REST.

INCIDENTALLY, CLASS ONLY STARTED TEN MINUTES AGO.
Z
Peirce

NATE, **WAKE UP!** YOU CAN'T SLEEP YOUR WAY THROUGH CLASS!
HM? MMPH! OH... SORRY.

I WAS JUST TRYING TO... Y'KNOW... RECHARGE.
WELL, FIND **ANOTHER** WAY TO "RECHARGE"!

OKAY... WELL... I'VE GOT SOME CHEEZ DOODLES HERE...

I'D GIVE YOU SOME, BUT I'M REALLY HUNGRY.
NARF NARF NARF NARF

NATE, THIS IS DANIEL, A NEW STUDENT. CAN YOU SHOW HIM AROUND?
WILL DO!

THAT'S MY LOCKER!
UH HUH.

RIGHT HERE IS WHERE I INVENTED MRS. GODFREY'S CLASSIC NICKNAME, "DULLAPALOOZA"!

THIS IS WHERE MR. GALVIN'S DENTURES FELL OUT WHILE HE WAS SCREAMING AT SETH QUINCY!

YOU'RE STANDING EXACTLY WHERE CHESTER BUDRICK GAVE RANDY BETANCOURT THE MOST EPIC WEDGIE OF ALL TIME!

AND HERE'S THE SPOT WHERE MARY ELLEN POPOWSKI BARFED LAST YEAR ON CINCO DE MAYO!

THERE! YOU'VE SEEN IT ALL! CATCH YOU LATER! MAYBE AT LUNCH!

EXCUSE ME, WHICH WAY TO THE CAFETERIA?
Peirce

PETER, HONEY? I'M OFF TO MY BOARD MEETING!
WHAT? WHY WASHN'T I INFORMED OF THISH?

I TOLD YOU ABOUT IT, SWEETIE. MAYBE YOU WEREN'T LISTENING.
YESH, BECAUSE I WASH READING! I WASH IMPROVING MY MIND!

WHEN I'M READING A WORK OF LITERATURE, I'M FOCUSHED LIKE A LASHER BEAM! NOTHING CAN BREAK MY CON–

PETER, M'BOY!
NYAH!
Peirce

WHAT ARE **YOU** DOING HERE?
BABYSITTING, OF COURSE! AND YOUR MOM WANTS YOU TO GET SOME **EXERCISE**!

SO WE'RE GOING TO THE POND! GET YOUR SKATES!
GROANN...

WHA-? THOSE ARE **FIGURE SKATES**!
SHO? WHAT'SH THE DIFFERENCE?

I'M HERE NOT A MOMENT TOO SOON.
WHY CAN'T YOU JUSHT LIE ON THE SHOFA AND WATCH "BRIDEZILLASH" LIKE OTHER BABYSITTERSH?
peirce

PETER, IT'S TIME FOR YOU TO LEARN ABOUT THE GREAT GAME OF **ICE HOCKEY**!
BUT I LOATHE SHPORTSH.

HOCKEY'S NOT JUST A SPORT, IT'S A WAY OF **LIFE**!
HERE, TAKE THIS.
WHAT ISH IT?

IT'S YOUR **STICK**, OBVIOUSLY! YOU USE IT TO PASS THE PUCK! TO SHOOT THE PUCK!

...AND, IN SPECIAL CASES, TO CLOCK PEOPLE UPSIDE THE HEAD.
GOOD HEAVENSH.

ISN'T THIS GREAT, PETER? DOESN'T THIS BEAT SITTING IN YOUR ROOM **READING**?
ARE YOU **SHERIOUSH**?

I'D **MUCH** RATHER READ! ESHPECIALLY THE BOOK I'M CURRENTLY ENJOYING!

"THE BROTHERS KARAMAZOV"!
THE BROTHERS KARA-?...HM...

ARE THOSE THE DUDES WHO MADE "THE MATRIX"?
CRIPESH.
Peirce

I SHLIPPED.
THAT'S OKAY, PETER! FALLING IS PART OF LEARNING TO SKATE!

THE **IMPORTANT** THING IS: WHEN A HOCKEY PLAYER FALLS DOWN, WHAT DOES HE DO?

HE WAITSH RIGHT HERE UNTIL A TURBO-HOT FIGURE SHKATER COMESH OVER TO OFFER HELP.

OOH, YOU POOR LITTLE GUY!
HI.
GOOD GAME PLAN.

OKAY, PETER, I THINK YOU'RE READY TO JOIN THAT PICK-UP GAME OVER THERE!
"PICK-UP"?

WHY ISH IT CALLED "PICK-UP"?

WHAM!

PICK ME UP.
SHAY! THISH ISH **EXHILAR-ATING!**

HEY, ISN'T THAT THE KID NATE BABYSITS?
YOU'RE RIGHT!

PETER?
WHAT'S WRONG?
SHNIFF!

WHERE'S NATE?
I DON'T KNOW! THAT'SH THE WHOLE PROBLEM!

HE WASH HERE, AND THEN HE JUSHT... LEFT!
HE DID?
SOB!

THAT IDIOT!
WHICH WAY DID HE GO, PETER?
TOWARD THAT SHED.

LET'S GO GIVE HIM A FACE-WASH!
YEAH! ANYONE WHO'D LEAVE A LITTLE KID ALL ALONE IS...

POW!
POW!

...ISH A TACTICAL GENIUSH!
THAT WAS TOO EASY.
Peirce

DAD, I FINISHED THE DISHES AND I'M DONE WITH MY HOMEWORK.
MM.

SO CAN I WATCH A LITTLE TV?
YES, YOU MAY.

UH-OH... NO... **NO!**...

NO!
SANDRA, THIS PROMISES TO BE THE MOST EXCITING DAY OF FIGURE SKATING IN A LONG, **LONG** TIME!
Peirce

ELLEN, WE'RE **NOT** GOING TO SIT HERE AND WATCH **FIGURE SKATING**! GIMME THE REMOTE!
NO!

FINE! I'LL CHANGE THE CHANNEL BY **HAND**!
...AND THIS IS THE BIGGEST JUMP OF HER ROUTINE, A TRIPLE-FLIP TRIPLE-TOE COMBINATION...

...AND SHE NAILS IT!

HOW ABOUT WE COMPROMISE AND HIT THE "MUTE" BUTTON?
WASN'T THAT **FABULOUS**, SANDRA?
I'VE GOT CHILLS, SCOTT!
Peirce

ELLEN, YOU WANT TO WATCH FIGURE SKATING, AND I WANT TO WATCH BASKETBALL. THERE'S A VERY SIMPLE SOLUTION.

WE CAN BOTH DVR OUR SHOWS AND WATCH THEM LATER, WHENEVER IT'S CONVENIENT!

OH, WAIT, I JUST REMEMBERED SOMETHING!
THUNK!

WE DON'T HAVE A DVR!!
KEEP IT UP AND WE WON'T HAVE A TV.
METRO/REGION
Peirce

DING DONG!
GO GET THAT, WILL YOU? I INVITED A FRIEND OVER TO WATCH SKATING.

GREAT. SO THERE'LL BE **TWO** OF YOU GIGGLING OVER SOME STUPID **ICE SHOW**!

!
Peirce

I CAN'T TAKE IT.
...AND NOW HERE'S SANDRA IN THE KISS-AND-CRY AREA...

OHH! THAT'S A BAD FALL, SANDRA!
SHE JUST COULDN'T PULL OFF THAT TRIPLE LUTZ, SCOTT!
! !

...AND THAT'S GOING TO TAKE HER OFF THE PODIUM!
THAT'S RIGHT, SCOTT. THERE'LL BE NO GOLD MEDAL TODAY!

SNIFF!
WHIMPER!

WAAH!
OWOOOOO

GORDIE, MY MAN!
HI, NATE! IS ELLEN HERE?

I THOUGHT SHE AND I COULD HANG OUT FOR A BIT!
I DON'T KNOW IF THAT'S SUCH A GOOD IDEA.

WHY? IS SHE SICK?

DEEPLY.
NO TALK-ING DURING FIGURE SKATING!
Peirce

WHAT'S UP, GUYS?
A BREAKTHROUGH, CHAD, MY BOY! A **BREAK-THROUGH!**

HUH?
WE ALL KNOW I'M AFRAID OF CATS, RIGHT?

RIGHT.
AND WE **ALSO** KNOW THAT HIT-TING MYSELF ON THE HEAD WITH AN EMPTY PLASTIC BOT-TLE **RELAXES** ME!
THUNK THUNK THUNK THUNK

I'M ABOUT TO PROVE THAT THE RELAXING POWER OF THE BOTTLE CAN **OVERRIDE** MY CAT PHOBIA!

WATCH CLOSELY, CHAD! YOU'RE ABOUT TO SEE **HISTORY** BEING MADE!
OKAY, FRANCIS, LET PICKLES OUT OF THE BASEMENT!
THUNK THUNK THUNK

HERE, KITTY... NICE KITTY...
THUNK THUNK THUNK THUNK THUNK

GAH!
FSSST!

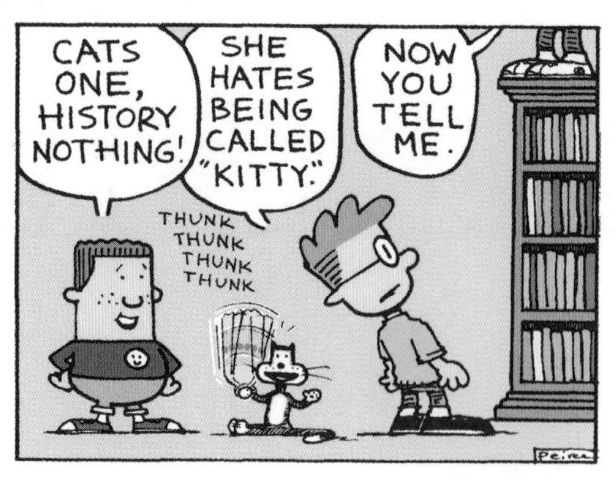
CATS ONE, HISTORY NOTHING!
SHE HATES BEING CALLED "KITTY."
NOW YOU TELL ME.
THUNK THUNK THUNK THUNK

GUYS, WE NEED A NAME.
UH... WE ALREADY **HAVE** NAMES, EINSTEIN.

I MEAN A **GROUP** NAME! FOR THE THREE OF US!
WHY DO WE NEED A NAME?

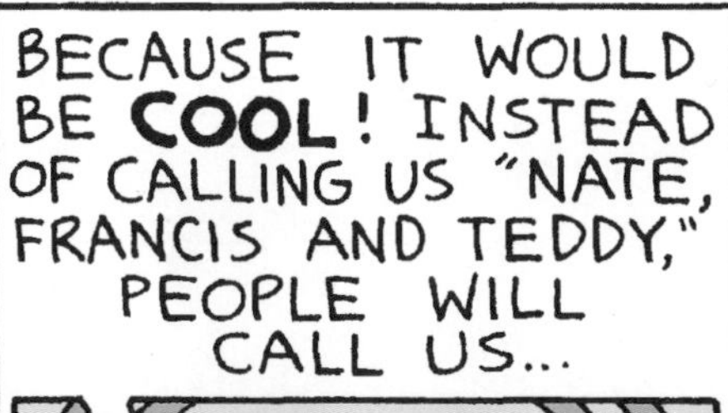
BECAUSE IT WOULD BE **COOL**! INSTEAD OF CALLING US "NATE, FRANCIS AND TEDDY," PEOPLE WILL CALL US...

"FRANCIS AND COMPANY"!
NO.
THAT SOUNDS LIKE A LAME SITCOM STARRING SCOTT BAIO.
Peirce

I HAD A BRAIN-STORM, BOYS! I KNOW EXACTLY WHAT WE SHOULD CALL OURSELVES!

WE'LL COMBINE THE FIRST LETTERS OF OUR LAST NAMES: POPE, ORTIZ, WRIGHT! GET IT?

POW!

WE GET IT.
NICE MOVE, DORKUS.
IBRARY
SOME BRAIN-STORMS ARE STORMIER THAN OTHERS.

SO IT'S OFFICIAL! FROM NOW ON, WE'RE CALLING OURSELVES **POW!**

WHEN PEOPLE SEE US, THEY'LL SAY "HERE COMES POW"!
WAIT, WILL THEY SAY "HERE COMES POW" OR "HERE **COME** POW"?

YEAH! DO YOU SAY THE UTAH JAZZ **IS** PLAYING WELL, OR THE UTAH JAZZ **ARE** PLAYING WELL?
IT'S THE WHOLE SINGULAR OR PLURAL QUESTION.

WELL, THEY'RE THE JAZZ, SO EVEN IF THEY **DO** PLAY WELL, THEY'LL PROBABLY PLAY LOUSY IN THE NEXT GAME.
SO TRUE.
GUYS! HEY! **FOCUS!**
Peirce

GINA, I'D LIKE TO INTRODUCE YOU TO **POW!**

WHAT?
FRANCIS, TEDDY AND I! THAT'S THE NAME OF OUR GROUP! WE'RE **POW!**

SNORT! YOU LOOK MORE LIKE **SNAP, CRACKLE, AND POP!**

OUCH.
MAYBE **SHE** SHOULD BE POW.
NO, I'VE GOT ANOTHER NAME FOR HER.
Peirce

EXCUSE ME, BOYS, WHICH ONE OF YOU IS "POW"?
HEAR THAT, GUYS? OUR NAME IS CATCH-ING ON!

POW IS WHAT THE THREE OF US CALL OURSELVES! WE'RE ALL POW!
I SEE.

THEN ALL OF YOU WILL GO TO DETENTION FOR WRITING "POW" ON THE TABLES IN THE COMPUTER LAB.

HE'S POW.
HEY!
Peirce

INVENTING A NAME FOR OURSELVES WENT OVER LIKE A LEAD BALLOON. NOBODY'S CALLING US "POW."
YEAH.

MAYBE WE SHOULD JUST LET **OTHER** PEOPLE DECIDE WHAT TO CALL US.

WELL, IF IT ISN'T THE THREE **DORKETEERS!**

OR MAYBE NOT.
I'M JUST GOING TO BE ANONYMOUS.
PEIRCE

WHAT ARE YOU WATCHING?
THE NEWS.

IF I WANT TO SEE WINK SUMMERS, MY FAVORITE TV METEOROLOGIST, I'VE GOT TO WATCH HIM ON **WEEKENDS**!

HOW COME?
BECAUSE HE GOT **DEMOTED**, THAT'S HOW COME!

THEY PUSHED HIM FROM PRIMETIME ON WEEKNIGHTS TO THE WEEKEND! FROM THE PENTHOUSE TO THE OUTHOUSE!

I MEAN, THAT'S **HUMILIATING**! YOU CAN'T GET MUCH LOWER THAN **THAT**!

...AND NOW IT'S TIME FOR A **NEW** FEATURE HERE ON CHANNEL 12 ACTION NEWS: WE CALL IT "**PETS DO THE WACKIEST THINGS**"!

JOINING US WITH THE ZANY STORY OF A VERY UNUSUAL CAT IS OUR OWN **WINK SUMMERS**! WINK?
THANKS, SANDRA!

YOU KNOW, **MOST** CATS DON'T ENJOY SKYDIVING...
YOU WERE SAYING?
POOR WINK.

HEY, GUYS, DID YOU HEAR? WE HAVE A SUB IN SCIENCE!
YES! THAT MEANS WE DON'T HAVE THE TEST!

NO, I HEARD SHE'S STILL GIVING US THE TEST.
WHAT? SHE CAN'T DO THAT!

THAT'S A TOTAL VIOLATION OF THE FIRST COMMANDMENT OF SUBSTITUTE TEACHING!

"THOU SHALT HAND OUT A LAME WORK-SHEET, THEN SPEND THE WHOLE PERIOD READING MAGAZINES."

WOWZA!

IS THERE **REALLY** A LIST OF COMMANDMENTS FOR SUBSTITUTE TEACHERS?
THERE **SHOULD** BE.

LIKE: THOU SHALT NOT HAVE ANY TEACHING EXPERIENCE WHATSOEVER!
YEAH!

OR: THOU SHALT NOT, WHEN TAKING ATTENDANCE, SAY TO A STUDENT "ARE YOU REALLY IN SIXTH GRADE? YOU LOOK SO **YOUNG!**"

...BECAUSE **SOME** PEOPLE ARE JUST **SMALL** FOR THEIR AGE, **OKAY?**
POOR CHAD.
PEIRCE

HEY, ARE YOU THE SCIENCE SUB?
YES, INDEED! I'M MRS. BRISTOW!

AND YOU'RE GIVING US A TEST, RIGHT?
ACCORDING TO MR. GALVIN'S INSTRUCTIONS, YES.

DURING THE TEST, IS IT OKAY IF I HIT MYSELF ON THE HEAD WITH THIS EMPTY PLASTIC BOTTLE TO RELIEVE STRESS?

THERE ARE SOME THINGS THEY DON'T TELL YOU AT SUB TRAINING.
OTHERWISE, I MIGHT FREAK OUT.
THUNK THUNK THUNK THUNK THUNK
Peirce

WE NEED TO BEGIN THIS TEST, YOUNG MAN. TAKE YOUR SEAT.
ARE YOU A SCIENTIST?

I MEAN, HOW COME THEY HIRED YOU TO BE A SCIENCE SUB? HOW MUCH DO YOU KNOW ABOUT SCIENCE?

I BELIEVE A MORE RELEVANT QUESTION IS: HOW MUCH DO **YOU** KNOW ABOUT SCIENCE?

...ANNNND BEGIN.
I HATE RELEVANT QUESTIONS.
Peirce

HOW CAN I CONCENTRATE ON THIS TEST WITH YOU MAKING THAT RACKET?
NOT MY PROB, GINA. I'M TREATING MY STRESS.
THUNK THUNK THUNK THUNK

YOUR STRESS? WHAT ABOUT MY STRESS? YOU AND THAT STUPID BOTTLE ARE MAKING ME INSANE!
HOW TRAGIC.
THUNK
THUNK

I'LL COMPLAIN TO THE TEACHER!
SHE ALREADY GAVE ME PERMISSION.
THUNK THUNK

ARRRGH!
BEST TEST EVER!
THUNK THUNK
THUNK
THUNK

THUNKA THUNK
THUNKA THUNKA
THUNK THUNK
THUNKA THUNKA
THUNKA

THUNKA THUNK THUNK
NKA THUNKA THUNKA TH
WHAPPITY WHAP WHAPP
PPITY WHAP THUNKA TH
NKA
THUNKA
ITY
TONK
PPITY
TONK
WHAP
WHAP
WHAPP
WHAPPA
BOMP
BOMP
BOMP
TONKITY
TONK
TONK
TH
THU
THU

OH... UH... I WAS DONE WITH THE TEST, SO I THOUGHT I'D WORK ON THE DRUM INTRO TO "SMELLS LIKE TEEN SPIRIT."

CIPAL
OBVIOUSLY NOT A GRUNGE FAN.
Peirce

THANK YOU, GINA, FOR THAT MARVELOUS REPORT ON THE YEAR 1865!

NATE WILL NOW SHARE **HIS** REPORT ON THE YEAR...
...1969!

AHEM! IN 1969, RICHARD NIXON WAS PRESIDENT, NEIL ARMSTRONG LANDED ON THE MOON, AND A BOX SEAT AT A RED SOX GAME COST $3.50.

TODAY, THAT SAME SEAT COSTS **$135!!** IN FACT, FENWAY PARK HAS THE MOST EXPENSIVE "NON-PREMIUM" TICKET PRICES IN ALL OF BASEBALL!

WHY? TO PAY ALL THE RIDICULOUS **PLAYER SALARIES!** I MEAN, WHY ARE WE SPENDING **13 MILLION BUCKS** A SEASON FOR **SHANE VICTORINO**?

AT LEAST WE'VE GOT A NEW MANAGER THIS YEAR! THE GUY WE HAD **LAST** SEASON WAS AN ABSOLUTE **CLOWN**!

THERE WAS A GAME IN TEXAS WHEN HE...

SIT DOWN!

BENCHED!
SHE'S PROBABLY A YANKEES FAN.

LOOK AT THIS! SOME ELEVEN-YEAR-OLD KID INVENTED A NEW KIND OF MICROCHIP, AND NOW HE'S A **GAZILLIONAIRE**!

I'M ELEVEN! WHY COULDN'T **I** DO THAT? WHY COULDN'T **I** COME UP WITH A GREAT INVENTION?

BECAUSE YOU'RE NOT BRIGHT ENOUGH.

...OR HAVE YOU FORGOTTEN YOUR IDEA FOR MONKEY-POWERED WINDMILLS?
IT COULD HAVE WORKED. I WAS SO **CLOSE**!
Peirce

MR. GALVIN, LET'S SAY I WANTED TO INVENT SOMETHING. HOW WOULD I GET STARTED?

WELL, AN INVENTOR USUALLY BEGINS BY IDENTIFYING A PROB-LEM, THEN FINDING A **SOLUTION** TO THAT PROBLEM.

SO I JUST NEED TO THINK OF A PROB-?
HEY! **HEY!** THAT'S **IT!**

GUYS! I'VE GOT A PROBLEM!
JUST ONE?

MR. GALVIN SAID INVENTORS START BY IDENTIFYING A PROBLEM, RIGHT?
RIGHT.

WELL, WHAT'S THE BIGGEST PROBLEM FACING THE WORLD TODAY?
UM... POLLUTION?

NOPE! THE ORANGE POWDER YOU GET ALL OVER YOUR FINGERS WHEN YOU EAT A BAG OF CHEEZ DOODLES!

THAT WAS GOING TO BE MY SECOND GUESS.
I WILL INVENT HISTORY'S FIRST **POWDER-FREE DOODLE!**
Peirce

BEHOLD THE CHEEZ DOODLE!
UH-HUH.

IF I WANT TO INVENT A POWDER-FREE CHEEZ DOODLE, THE FIRST STEP IS TO DETERMINE WHAT THIS LITTLE BABY LOOKS LIKE **UNDER** THE POWDER!

OKAY, GIVE IT HERE. I'LL WASH IT OFF.
WHA-? **WASH** IT? NO **WAY**! WHY WASTE THE POWDER?

SUCKA SUCKA SUCKA SUCKA SUCKA SUCKA
GROSS ME OUT.
Peirce

WHAT'S THAT?
IT'S THE NEW CHEEZ DOODLE PROTOTYPE I INVENTED!

HOW COME IT'S NOT ORANGE?
BECAUSE INSTEAD OF COATING THE OUTSIDE WITH CHEESE POWDER, I PUT THE CHEESE ON THE INSIDE!

TRY IT!
OKAY.
CRUNCH!

HNNGGK!
IS THE TEXTURE OKAY? ALL I HAD WAS COTTAGE CHEESE.

STILL TRYING TO RE-INVENT THE CHEEZ DOODLE?
NOPE. I'VE BEEN STYMIED.

IT'S TOO HARD TO INJECT THE FLAVORING INSIDE THE DOODLE! IT'S IMPOSSIBLE!

THE ONLY SOLUTION IS TO GET RID OF THE DOODLE AL-TOGETHER, LEAVING THE DELICIOUS TASTE TO STAND **ALONE**!

SO YOU INVENTED... CHEESE?
GRANTED, IT'S NOT QUITE THE BREAKTHROUGH I'D HOPED FOR...
Peirce

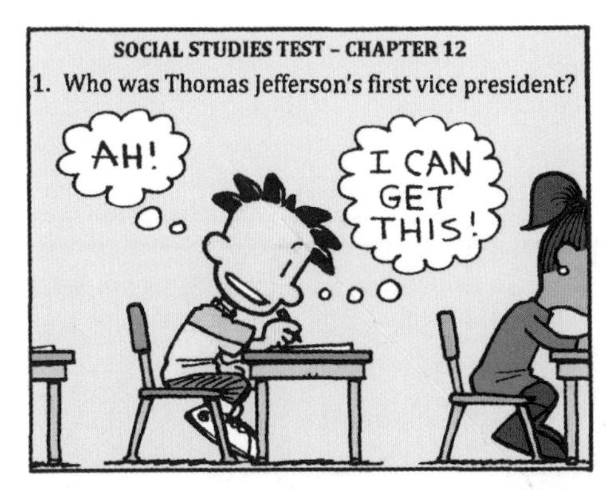
SOCIAL STUDIES TEST – CHAPTER 12
1. Who was Thomas Jefferson's first vice president?
AH!
I CAN GET THIS!

THOMAS JEFFERSON REMINDS ME OF JEFFERSON AIRPLANE! WHAT WAS ONE OF THEIR BIGGEST HITS? "WHITE RABBIT!"

WHO'S THE WORLD'S MOST FAMOUS RABBIT? BUGS BUNNY! WHAT DOES BUGS BUNNY EAT? CARROTS!

WHAT COLOR ARE CARROTS? ORANGE! WHAT RHYMES WITH ORANGE? NOTHING!

WHAT'S THE NUMERICAL EQUIVALENT OF NOTHING? ZERO! WHEN THE TEMPERATURE'S ZERO, HOW'S THE WEATHER? COLD!

WHEN THE WEATHER'S COLD, WHAT DO PEOPLE SAY? BRRR! WHAT'S ANOTHER WAY TO SPELL IT? BURR!

JEFFERSON'S FIRST VICE PRESIDENT WAS AARON BURR!

2. When was
surrende
TIME'S UP, PEOPLE! HAND 'EM IN!
!

IT MAY BE TIME FOR A NEW SYSTEM.
WHAT DID YOU PUT FOR QUESTION 10?

...AND WE END OUR BROADCAST TONIGHT WITH SOME SAD NEWS: CHIEF METEOROLOGIST **CHIP CAVENDISH** IS LEAVING CHANNEL 12 ACTION NEWS!
!

BUT IT'S FOR A GOOD REASON! RIGHT, CHIP?
RIGHT, DONNA! I'VE TAKEN A JOB AT A TV STATION IN ATLANTA, MY HOME-TOWN!

GOOD LUCK, CHIP! AND TAKING CHIP'S PLACE IS A FRIEND WE ALL KNOW WELL... OUR ONCE **AND** FUTURE CHIEF METEOROLOGIST...

...WINK SUMMERS!
YES!
Peirce

WHAT'S ALL THE SHOUTING?
DAD, **LOOK**! WINK SUMMERS WAS REINSTATED AS CHIEF METEOROLOGIST!

WELCOME BACK TO PRIME TIME, WINK!
THANKS, DONNA, I'M THRILLED TO BE HERE!

...BUT BEFORE I LOOK AT TONIGHT'S WEATHER, I'D LIKE TO APOLOGIZE FOR HOW BADLY I SCREWED UP LAST WEEKEND'S FORECAST!

I HONESTLY DIDN'T SEE THOSE MUDSLIDES COMING.
HE HASN'T CHANGED A BIT!
peirce

NOW LET'S LOOK AT THE FIVE-DAY FORECAST...
WHY ARE YOU SUCH A FAN OF WINK SUMMERS?

BECAUSE HE'S COOL, DAD! HE'S NOT ONE OF THOSE PHONY BALONEY, BLOW-DRIED METEOROLOGISTS! WINK'S A REGULAR GUY! HE'S AN EVERYMAN!

...AND BY FRIDAY, THIS WARM FRONT WILL... BELLCH!

WOO! PARDON MY CHILI!
SEE? THAT'S REAL!
Peirce

...AND THAT'S YOUR FIRST LOOK AT TONIGHT'S WEATHER! BUT BEFORE I SIGN OFF, I'D LIKE TO THANK ALL MY FANS OUT THERE FOR THEIR SUPPORT!

YOUR CARDS, LETTERS, AND EMAILS KEPT MY SPIRITS UP DURING A **VERY** DIFFICULT TIME IN MY LIFE!

IT'S NOT EASY WHEN YOUR BOSS SAYS, "WINK, THE FOCUS GROUPS TELL US THAT VIEWERS WANT A **DIFFERENT** KIND OF METEOROLOGIST!"

WELL, EX**CUSE** ME, BUT WHAT DOES A STINKIN' **FOCUS GROUP** KNOW ABOUT THE **WEATHER**??
WINK, I THINK IT'S TIME FOR A COMMERCIAL...
Peirce

HELLO, IS THIS CHIEF METEOROLOGIST WINK SUMMERS?
WINK! NUMBER ONE FAN NATE WRIGHT HERE!

CONGRATULATIONS ON GETTING YOUR OLD JOB BACK, WINK! I'VE WATCHED YOU EVERY NIGHT THIS WEEK, AND YOUR FORECASTS HAVE BEEN AWESOME!

AWESOME IN TERMS OF AESTHETICS, WINK, NOT ACCURACY.

SAY, WINK, NOW THAT YOUR PROFESSIONAL LIFE IS BACK ON TRACK, MAYBE YOU CAN GET YOUR **PERSONAL** LIFE ROLLING AGAIN!

YOUR WIFE DUMPED YOU WHEN YOU LOST YOUR JOB, RIGHT? WELL, I'LL BET **NOW** SHE'LL...

WHAT? SHE DID **WHAT**? AL**READY**? TO **WHO**?

SHE MARRIED THE **SPORTS ANCHOR**?
THE JOCKS ALWAYS GET THE GIRLS.

WANNA GO OVER THE SOCIAL STUDIES?
HIT ME!

WHAT YEAR DID JOHN ADAMS DIE?
1843!

NOPE.
RATS!

HOW FAR OFF WAS I?
SEVENTEEN YEARS.

OKAY... LET'S SEE HERE... THAT WOULD BEEEEE...

...1816!

AFTER THIS, HOW ABOUT WE WORK ON YOUR MATH?
NO, WAIT! 1870!
PEIRCE

HI, MRS. SHIPULSKI!
HELLO, BOYS. HERE TO SEE PRINCIPAL NICHOLS?

NOPE, WE'RE HERE TO SEE **YOU**!
REALLY? WHY'S THAT?

BECAUSE WE **LIKE** YOU, OF COURSE! BECAUSE WE ENJOY SPENDING TIME WITH YOU, AND LISTENING TO YOUR STORIES, AND...

...AND BECAUSE YOU KEEP A JAR OF JELLY BEANS IN YOUR MMPH!
I'LL HANDLE THIS, CHAD.
Peirce

ALL RIGHT, BOYS... YOU MAY EACH HAVE FIVE JELLY BEANS.
YAY!
THANKS!

I WANT A LIME ONE, BUT HOW DO I KNOW IF THIS GREEN ONE IS LIME? IT MIGHT BE SOUR APPLE, AND I **HATE** SOUR APPLE!

SMELL IT AND SEE.

SNIFFA SNIFFA SNIFFA
SNIFFA SNUFFA SNUFFA
SNUFF SNUFF SNORT
SNIFFA SNIFFA SNIFFA
SNUFFA SNUFF SNIFF

CAN'T TELL. I'M PUTTIN' IT BACK.
NO, YOU'RE NOT.

CHOMPF! CHOMPF! NO!... NO!
WHAT'S THE MATTER?
! !

THE JELLY BEAN I JUST ATE! IT WAS RED, BUT IT WAS WATERMELON!

RED JELLY BEANS SHOULD BE CHERRY! WATERMELON SHOULDN'T EVEN BE A JELLY BEAN FLAVOR!

ARTIFICIAL WATERMELON FLAVORING IS AN ABOMINATION!
CHAD'S A CANDY PURIST.
PEIRCE

HERE'S THE ISSUE: LEMON JELLY BEANS TASTE LIKE LEMONS. LIME JELLY BEANS TASTE LIKE LIMES.

...BUT **WATERMELON** JELLY BEANS TASTE **NOTHING** LIKE WATERMELONS! NOT EVEN **CLOSE**!

NAME ME **ONE** ARTIFICIAL FRUIT FLAVOR THAT TASTES **LESS** LIKE THE REAL THING!
WED.

GRAPE?
OOH. THAT'S GOOD.

WHAT'S ALL THIS?
I'M TRYING TO FIND OUT WHAT'S THE MOST POPULAR JELLY BEAN FLAVOR!

I'VE LINED UP JELLY BEANS OF EVERY POSSIBLE FLAVOR ON THIS TABLE!

THEN I'LL RECORD WHICH FLAVOR EVERY-BODY IN THE CLASS CHOOSES FIRST!

GOOD LUCK WITH THAT.
HEY!
SORRY, CHAD.
MUNCH MUNCH MUNCH MUNCH

WHAT'S YOUR FAVORITE JELLY BEAN FLAVOR?
LEMON!

WHAT'S YOUR FAVORITE JELLY BEAN FLAVOR?
ORANGE!

WHAT'S YOUR FAVORITE JELLY BEAN FLAVOR?
I CAN'T STAND JELLY BEANS.

TOLD YA.
THAT'S JUST WRONG.

TOMORROW'S APRIL FOOL'S DAY.
YEAH. SO?

SO ARE YOU GONNA PLAY SOME STUPID TRICK ON ME?
TOMORROW? NOPE.

I **THOUGHT** ABOUT IT. I THOUGHT ABOUT WHAT KIND OF TRICK WOULD CATCH YOU OFF GUARD.

BUT YOU KNOW ME TOO WELL. YOU UNDERSTAND ALL MY TRICK-PLAYING PATTERNS.

EVENTUALLY, I DECIDED THERE WAS NO WAY TO PLAY AN APRIL FOOL'S TRICK ON YOU WITHOUT YOU SEEING IT COMING.

KLIK!

WHAM

...UNLESS I STARTED A DAY EARLY.

GUESS WHO'S GOING TO BE THE ASSISTANT COACH OF YOUR LITTLE LEAGUE TEAM THIS YEAR!
NOT COACH JOHN!

PLEASE TELL ME IT'S NOT COACH JOHN! PLEASE PLEASE PLEASE! ANYONE BUT COACH JOHN!

RELAX, NATE! IT'S NOT COACH JOHN! IT'S ME!

GREAT NEWS, RIGHT?
OKAY, WHEN I SAID "ANYONE BUT COACH JOHN," WHAT I MEANT WAS...

I'M READY FOR PRACTICE.
CHEER UP, NATE! YOU LOOK LIKE YOU'RE GOING TO A FUNERAL!

DON'T WANT ME TO BE THE ASSISTANT COACH, EH? AFRAID I'LL EMBARRASS YOU?

WELL, THERE'S NOTHING WRONG WITH A LITTLE EMBARRASSMENT! IT TEACHES YOU HOW TO COPE WITH THINGS!

I PLAY ON A TEAM CALLED THE "CREAM PUFFS." I'VE COPED ENOUGH.

I'VE GOT A MAJOR **SURPRISE**, TEAM! YOU'RE GOING TO NOTICE SOMETHING **DIFFERENT** THIS YEAR!
COACH

WE'RE NOT CALLED THE "CREAM PUFFS" ANYMORE???
WOO-HOO!
YEAH!
YAAY!
AWESOME!!
COAC

NO, WE'RE STILL THE CREAM PUFFS... BUT WE'VE GOT **NATE'S DAD** AS OUR ASSISTANT COACH! GIVE HIM A HAND!
COACH

WAIT, WHO?
CLAP.
HI, KIDS.
COAC

OKAY, GANG! I'LL GIVE YOU THE SITUATION, AND YOU MAKE THE PLAY!

BASES LOADED, ONE OUT!

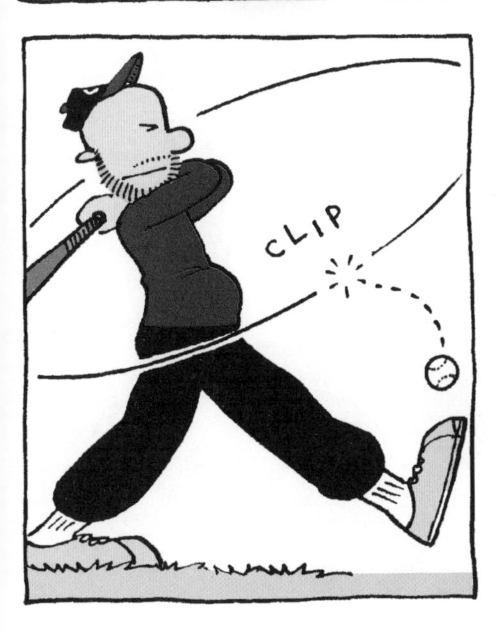
CLIP

HEH HEH... PRACTICE SWING!
MOMENTS LIKE THIS MAKE ME GRATEFUL THAT MY DAD SHOWS NO INTEREST IN MY LIFE.
Peirce

OKAY, HERE WE GO! HOT GROUNDER!

POW!

OW!

ID IT BOKEN?
NICE ONE, DAD.
Peirce

WHOOPS! SORRY 'BOUT THAT!

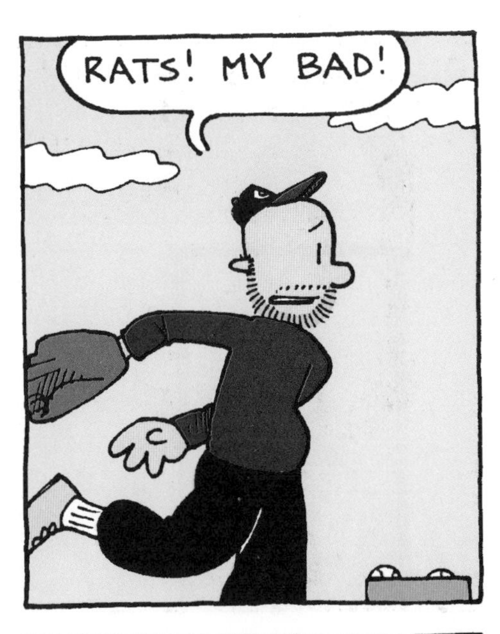
RATS! MY BAD!

I'LL TAKE IT FROM HERE, MARTY.
OH. OKAY.
COA

YOU DON'T OFTEN SEE A RELIEF PITCHER DURING BATTING PRACTICE.
SIGH...
peirce

HOMEWORK, NATE.
OKAY, OKAY.

Due: April 8th
Describe a time in your life when you became ANGRY or FRUSTRATED. What prompted these feelings? How did you respond to them?

I remember one time, our English teacher gave us the lamest homework assignment ever.

As usual, she told us to write about our FEELINGS instead of letting us make up stories about stuff we're actually INTERESTED in.

Plus, it was practically the exact same assignment she gave us LAST week.

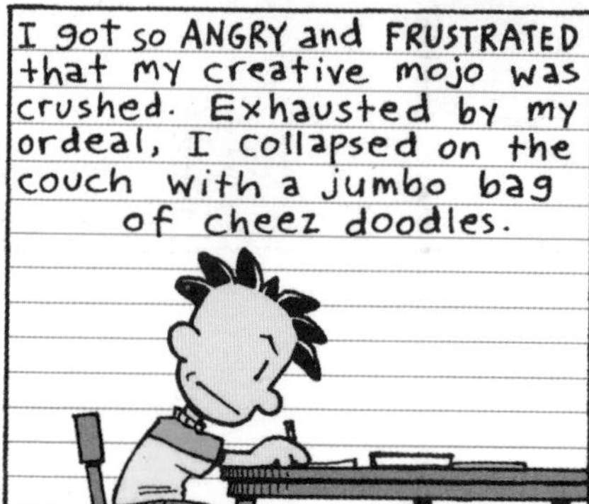
I got so ANGRY and FRUSTRATED that my creative mojo was crushed. Exhausted by my ordeal, I collapsed on the couch with a jumbo bag of cheez doodles.

DONE ALREADY?
YUP.

BIG SOCIAL STUDIES TEST THIS WEEK! WE'D BETTER START STUDYING!
UGH.

I HATE STUDYING SOCIAL STUDIES! MY BRAIN CAN'T REMEMBER NAMES AND DATES!

WHO THREW THE ONLY PERFECT GAME IN MONTREAL EXPOS HISTORY?
DENNIS MARTINEZ. JULY 28TH, 1991.

YOU WERE SAYING ABOUT YOUR BRAIN?
BUT THAT'S BASEBALL! THAT'S IMPORTANT!
Peirce

YOU KNOW WHAT YOUR PROBLEM IS? YOUR BRAIN ONLY REMEMBERS STUFF YOU'RE **INTERESTED** IN!
NO **KIDDING**, FRANCIS!

THAT'S HOW **EVERYONE'S** BRAIN WORKS! YOU FILTER OUT THE GARBAGE SO YOU CAN FOCUS ON THE **GOOD** STUFF!
WHAT'S THE GOOD STUFF?

SPORTS STATS, TV AND MOVIE QUOTES, COMICS, SNACK FOODS, SONG LYRICS, VIDEO GAMES, AND "LORD OF THE RINGS" TRIVIA.

VERY HELPFUL FOR STUDYING FRANKLIN PIERCE.
WHO?
Peirce

HERE'S THE PLAN: YOUR BRAIN ONLY REMEMBERS STUFF YOU'RE ACTUALLY INTERESTED IN...

SO ALL WE HAVE TO DO IS UNCOVER SOME FACTS THAT MAKE SOCIAL STUDIES MORE INTERESTING!
FLIP
FLIP

AH-**HA**!

WHAT IF I TOLD YOU HERBERT HOOVER'S FIRST JOB WAS PICK-ING BUGS OFF POTATO PLANTS?
WHAT IF I IGNORED YOU AND PLAYED ANGRY BIRDS?
TIK
TIK
TIK
Peirce

THE WAY I SEE IT, THERE'S A LIMIT TO HOW MUCH INFORMATION A BRAIN CAN STORE.

EVERY TIME YOU TELL ME SOME RANDOM SOCIAL STUDIES FACT, MY BRAIN HAS TO MAKE ROOM FOR IT BY **FORGETTING** SOMETHING ELSE!

SO IF I TELL YOU THAT ELI WHITNEY INVENTED THE COTTON GIN IN 1793...
ARGH!

WHAT?
I JUST LOST SEASON 6, EPISODE 3 OF "STAR TREK: THE NEXT GENERATION."

LOOK, NATE, YOU CAN REMEMBER SPORTS TRIVIA AND STUFF LIKE THAT, SO CLEARLY YOU CAN REMEMBER HISTORICAL FACTS IF YOU TRY!

YOU JUST HAVE TO FOCUS. GOT IT?
FOCUS. GOT IT.

FOCUS.
FOCUS.

OKAY, WHAT YEAR DID THE U.S. SIGN THE TREATY OF...
I'M GONNA GRAB A SNACK. YOU WANT ANYTHING?

WHEN WAS THE BATTLE OF TIPPECANOE?
HOW SHOULD I KNOW?

ALL THIS HISTORY GARBAGE HAS NOTHING TO DO WITH MY LIFE! GIVE ME ONE REASON WHY I NEED TO REMEMBER THIS STUFF!

BECAUSE IF YOU FAIL THIS TEST, YOU'RE GOING TO SPEND EIGHT WEEKS IN SUMMER SCHOOL WITH MRS. GODFREY.

NOW. WHEN WAS THE BATTLE OF TIP–
NOVEMBER 7TH, 1811
PEIRCE

Big Nate is distributed internationally by Andrews McMeel Syndication.

Andrews McMeel Publishing
a division of Andrews McMeel Universal
1130 Walnut Street, Kansas City, Missouri 64106

www.andrewsmcmeel.com

18 19 20 21 22 SDB 11 10 9 8 7 6 5 4 3

ISBN: 978-1-4494-6229-1

Library of Congress Control Number: 2016945096

Made by:
Shenzhen Donnelley Printing Company Ltd.
Address and location of manufacturer:
No. 47, Wuhe Nan Road, Bantian Ind. Zone,
Shenzhen China, 518129
3rd Printing—1/15/18

These strips appeared in newspapers from
October 14, 2012, through April 13, 2013.

Big Nate can be viewed on the Internet at
www.gocomics.com/big_nate

Check out these and other books from Andrews McMeel Publishing

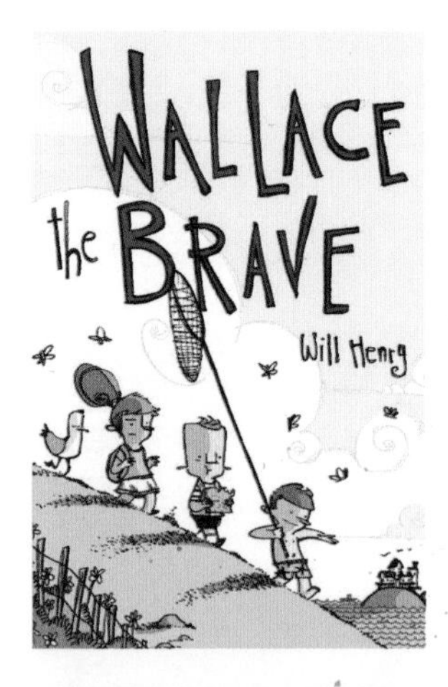